D1538493

The
Alphabet Game

The
Alphabet Game
Trina Schart Hyman

Books of Wonder
SeaStar Books
New York

Library of Congress Cataloging-in-Publication Data is available.

The art for this book was prepared using pen-and-ink and watercolors.
The text for this book is set in 10-point Garamond Italic.

ISBN 1-58717-008-6 (trade binding) 10 9 8 7 6 5 4 3 2 1

Printed in the United States of America.

Books of Wonder is a registered trademark of Ozma, Inc.

For more information about our books, and
the authors and artists who create them,
visit our web site: www.northsouth.com

To John Grandits
with affection
and gratitude
—T. S. H.

artist   artichoke   apples   ant

apron arm anemone acorns avocado

apron arm anemone acorns avocado

artist artichoke apples ant

brambles basket berries bees

beehive bird boy barefoot

beehive bird boy barefoot brow

bees beehive bird boy barefoot

buckle brambles basket berries

clouds curls cat crocus cage

cape cheek cake cricket canary

clouds curls cat crocus cage cape cheek

collar candle cheeks clouds

dog daffodil dirt dungarees

dandelion dragonfly daisies dig

dandelion dragonfly daisies dig

dog daffodil dirt dungarees

elbow   Easter basket   eyebrow

eat

eye

evening primrose

eyebrow   evening primrose

Easter basket   elbow   ear

egg

eat

eye

evening primrose

eggcup

frog pond fern fins

fish frayed float foot fly fist

frog pond fern fins fish frayed

fishing pole fingers feather

grapevine glass grass gnome

goose grapes geranium grasp girl

goose grapes geranium grasp girl

grapevine glass grass gnome

hay hole hawk halter hat

horse honeysuckle house bay

hole hawk halter hat horse

honeysuckle house bay hole

honeysuckle house bay hole

icicles ink ice skates island ice

ladybug lace lizard lollipop

lily lantern lashes

lily lantern lashes lean lemon lick

lizard lollipop lily lantern lashes

leaves lips lime ladybug lace

mouth mushrooms mist mouse

mosquito milkweed

mosquito milkweed marsh moon

mist mouse mosquito milkweed

moth marsh mouth mushrooms

navel nightingale nest nose

nixie nasturtium nuts net naked

nixie nasturtium nuts net naked

navel nightingale nest nose

on ocean oak orange owl on ocean oak orange owl on ocean oak orange owl on ocean oak orange owl on ocean oak orange owl on ocean oak

plum paddle pie pineapple

pinecone pan peaks plum paddle

percolator porcupine plaid pond

pear perch pine trees pack

quince Queen Anne's lace quilt

queen quilt Queen Anne's lace

queen quince Queen Anne's lace

queen quince

rabbit   ribbon   roller skates

race   raincoat   roses   race   rain

rabbit   ribbon   roller skates

race   raincoat   roses   race   rain

sea urchin   sandal   swimsuit

scallop starfish sea urchin sandal

sea sun spine sail seaweed sit

sand stick seagull sunglasses

table telephones toes talk

turtle topknots teeth tablecloth

tulips two teapot thread twist

twins ties tail top teacup

uncombed   under   umbrella

upon ups-a-daisies underwear

uncombed under umbrella

upon ups-a-daisies underwear

vegetables   village   valentine

violets vest valley vegetables violet

valley vegetables violets village

village valentine violets vest

water windmill weeds

wheelbarrow wade whistle

wheel wings water windmill

wood wind wren water lily

yarrow   yarn   Yorkshire terrier

yellow jackets   yawn   yarrow   yarn

Yorkshire terrier   yellow jackets

yawn   yarrow   yarn   Yorkshire terrier

zipper zinnia zoo zipper zinnia

zinnia zoo zipper zinnia zoo zipper zinnia zoo zipper